Tangled In The Bay
The Story of a Baby Right Whale

by Deborah Tobin
Illustrated by Jeffrey C. Domm

NIMBUS
PUBLISHING

For Moe Brown and Todd Sollows, with special thanks to Phil Hamilton, Amy Knowlton, Scott Kraus, and all the other scientists and conservationists whose work and dedication represent the right whale's best hope for a future.
Deborah Tobin

To my two sons, Lukas and Jakob, and a special thank you to my wife, Kristin, who has helped tremendously in the design and format of this book series.
Jeffrey C. Domm

Nimbus Publishing Limited
PO Box 9166
Halifax, NS   B3K 5M8
(902) 455-4286

Design: Jeffrey C. Domm
Photo Credits: p.30 Upper jaw and baleen of a right whale being hoisted aboard, from *Following the Sea*, by Benjamin Doane; p.32, Lisa Congor; p.32, Center for Coastal Studies; back cover photo of author, Judy Amirault; back cover of illustrator, Kristin B. Domm.

Printed and bound in China

National Library of Canada Cataloguing in Publication

>Tobin, Deborah
>Tangled in the bay : the story of a baby right whale / by Deborah Tobin ;
>illustrated by Jeffrey C. Domm.
>(Natural heroes)
>ISBN 1-55109-441-X

1. Balaena glacialis—Juvenile literature. 2. Animal rescue—Fundy, Bay of—Juvenile literature. I. Domm, Jeff, 1958- II. Title. III. Series.

QL737.C423T62 2003   j639.97'95273   C2003-900428-7

We acknowledge the financial support of the Government of Canada through the Book Publishing Industry Development Program (BPIDP) and the Canada Council for our publishing activities.

Natural Heroes
People Helping Animals

Extinction of animals has always been thought of as a natural process—but only at a rate of one species out of a million per century. Today, the rate could be as high as several species per day.

Around the world, individuals are helping to protect various species from extinction. Over 500 species and subspecies of plants and animals in North America have gone the way of the dodo bird; among them, the passenger pigeon, Audubon's bighorn sheep, the labrador duck, and the Eskimo curlew. Many more are facing extinction, including the North Atlantic right whale, whooping crane, piping plover, red wolf, woodland caribou, and even the beloved polar bear. From the wooded forests of the northwest through the prairies and across to the Atlantic coast, habitats are being destroyed at an alarming rate. **Natural Heroes** is a book series for children that explores the work of scientists, naturalists, researchers, biologists and everyday people who care enough about animals to take action in their defense. Without the help of these concerned people, we would lose many more species.

Tangled In The Bay: The Story of a Baby Right Whale is the first in a series of books written for children that explore the real-life situations these natural heroes face everyday when rescuing animals. We cannot save endangered animals from extinction without them.

Jeffrey C. Domm
Illustrator

$\mathcal{J}$t started out as a great day.

As our small white plane flew over the Bay of Fundy,
I watched its shadow glide easily among the porpoises
and dolphins in the water below. All the sea creatures,
from giant whales to tiny seabirds, were returning from their
winter homes. In Fundy's rich cold waters they would be busy
feeding for the next few months, fattening up for another winter.

We were busy as well, criss-crossing the Bay in search of rare
North Atlantic right whales.

"Let's fly lower," I called to Jack, the pilot,
as I strained to see into the water below. Our job
was to locate and count right whales on their feeding grounds
in the Bay of Fundy. Using this information, the Coast Guard
would warn ships crossing the Bay to steer clear of the whales.

Suddenly, cutting through the static in our earphones,
an urgent message came over the radio. "There's a young whale
tangled up in some fishing gear! The mother whale is trying to help!"
The worried voice belonged to Roy, a local fisherman. He told us
his location and said he would stay with the whales until we arrived.
Our great day had suddenly turned bad.

Jack opened the throttle and turned the plane toward the troubled whale.

We circled low, trying to spot the fisherman's boat.

"There," I said, pointing. A mother right whale and her calf lay close together not far from the boat. My heart sank as I recognized the pair. It was Clio and her calf, Pasha. Only six months ago Pasha had been born in the warm waters off the coast of Florida. Researchers had photographed the mother and calf before they set out on their journey to the Bay of Fundy. Now Pasha was hopelessly tangled in a strong fishing net that tugged against his shiny wet skin. He struggled bravely to get free, rolling and twisting his fat round body. But his struggle only made matters worse—the net was pulling tighter and tighter!

We didn't know how long Pasha had been tangled or how badly he was hurt. But we did know that this baby right whale was going to need help, and fast!

Untangling whales is dangerous work and requires special training and equipment. We couldn't help Pasha by ourselves. Whale rescuers would have to be flown in by Coast Guard helicopter from Cape Cod. We knew just who to call. David and Stormy had saved other whales. If anyone could untangle Pasha, they could. We radioed the Coast Guard and soon they were on their way. We let Roy know that we were flying back to shore but would return by boat as quickly as we could. We would wait with the whales until the Coast Guard arrived with David and Stormy.

We didn't waste a minute landing our plane and climbing aboard the boat that was standing by. When we returned to the whales, Pasha was still struggling. Even though Pasha's mother, Clio, must have been frightened and confused, she didn't leave her baby's side.

We watched and waited for the Coast Guard to arrive. It was difficult to see Pasha struggling without being able to help him. Time seemed to stand still until the rescuers arrived a few hours later.

We waved to David and Stormy as the Coast Guard boat approached. Dressed in bright orange survival suits, they launched an inflatable boat filled with equipment they had brought with them. I held my breath as the brave rescuers quietly rowed toward the whales.

David and Stormy would have to figure out how to untangle the calf without getting hurt themselves. Baby Pasha was as big as a pickup truck, and his wild struggle with the net was churning the water like a giant washing machine. Pasha was only a baby but already he was learning about the dangers around him. Perhaps for the first time he was frightened. I was frightened too.

As the afternoon wore on, we were so intent on freeing Pasha that we didn't notice the gathering storm clouds. In the Bay of Fundy, weather can become dangerous without any warning. The sky grew darker and the wind blew harder, lifting the small inflatable rescue boat higher and higher on the waves. The rescue would have to be called off for now. A bad day had just gotten worse.

There was one important job to do before we left the frightened whales.

Bracing against the force of the wind, Stormy carefully fastened
a radio tag to the rope that trailed from Pasha. Without a radio signal
it woud be very difficult to locate the whales after the storm.

Sadly, we returned to shore. There was nothing else we could do
for now, except wait and hope.

*T*hat night, friends and other whale rescuers came to my house in Freeport on Long Island. The howling wind drove the rain in from the darkness each time someone opened the door. We listened closely to the radio for weather reports and made plans for the next day. If the weather improved, we would try to rescue Pasha in the morning.

As I looked out the window at the rain pouring down
and the giant branches bending in the wind, all I could think
about was Pasha, trapped and tangled in the fishing gear.
My heart sent out a message to the baby whale:
Hold on a little longer, Pasha; we're coming back to help.

Dawn broke after a long, sleepless night. Thankfully the sea had calmed and the early morning sky was crystal clear. We had already left the wharf by the time the sun peeked above the horizon. A school of dolphins bounded in front of the boat as though leading us to their tangled ocean friend. Using our binoculars from atop the boat's wheelhouse, we searched the Bay for a sign of the whales. David sat close to the radio receiver. He was listening intently with earphones for the signal from Pasha's tag.

We scanned the endless expanse of glistening blue water.
The whales could be anywhere, moving with the surging tides
of the Bay of Fundy. Although we sighted many other whales—
rights, humpbacks, fins and minkes—there was no sign of Pasha
and his mother. We became more and more worried with each hour
that passed. Where could they be?

Suddenly, David's shout of excitement brought everyone running from all decks.
He was receiving a signal from the radio tag. Pasha and Clio were close!
Using the VHF radio, we contacted Jack in the airplane. He soon spotted the
whales and gave us their position.

Cautiously, we approached the whales. They lay quiet and still.
The only movement we could see was the opening and closing of
Clio's blowholes as she breathed slowly. Pasha wasn't moving at all.
Fearing the worst, we inched closer.

After a few frightening moments we saw a fine mist rise from
Pasha's blowholes. He made a faint hollow whispering sound
as he breathed. Pasha was alive but tired and weak from fighting
with the net for so long. Immediately, David and Stormy went to
work cutting the fishing gear. There was no time to lose. We kept a
close watch on Clio as the rescuers worked. She stayed near her baby,
alert and anxious.

Then, without warning, she raised her tail fluke high into the air.

We froze. The fluke could easily crush the rescuers in their small inflatable boat. What was she doing?

The giant tail smacked the water again and again, soaking David and Stormy and splashing icy cold seawater into their boat. Suddenly, Clio's fluke tip caught a piece of net already loosened by the rescuers. As Pasha's mother swung her powerful tail away from the calf, she lifted the net and flung it into the air. Pasha was free!

But still, the baby whale didn't stir. His mother nudged him gently with her head again and again, urging him to move.

Silently, we waited.

At first, Pasha's body appeared lifeless, but slowly he began to respond to his mother's touch. He stretched this way and that, testing his new freedom with growing strength. Then, as we watched, Pasha and his mother raised their flukes as if waving goodbye and vanished beneath the surface of the ocean.

David and Stormy worked quickly to pull the net and rope aboard so that other whales wouldn't get caught. With the pile of net stowed safely at the stern, we steered toward home, tired but happy.

As we moved through the water, I searched the sea behind us, but there was no sign of the whales.

Goodbye for now, Pasha, I whispered to the waves.
Keep safe.

History

The North Atlantic right whale is the rarest large whale species in the world—fewer than 325 remain. Early whalers first named them that because they were thought to be the "right whale" to kill. Right whale carcasses float, so whalers had an easy time recovering harpooned whales. The whales were hunted for their valuable supply of baleen and blubber. Baleen was used to make buggy whips, corset stays, and even wigs. The oil derived from blubber was used to fuel street lamps and to make soap. Because they were

such a popular target for whalers for so many years, right whale populations became scarcer and scarcer. In 1935, when the hunting of right whales was stopped, scientists believed that as few as one hundred remained.

Current Threats

Although right whales are now safe from whalers, they continue to face threats from other human activities. Sometimes right whales die from collisions with ships and are often injured, as Pasha could have been, by entanglements with fishing gear. Such deaths and injuries are accidental and scientists are working to discover ways to prevent them. For instance, it might be possible to find a way to warn whales that a ship is coming, or that a net is nearby, so they can swim out of the way. In the meantime, some researchers are working hard to let ships know where the whales are so that they can avoid hitting them, and others are working with fishermen to solve the entanglement problem.

Description

The average North Atlantic right whale is 12-15 metres (40-50 feet) long and weighs about 45 tonnes (100,000 pounds). Its shape is rather unusual; the head is one-quarter of the body length, and the girth (measured around the belly) is about two-thirds of its total length. In other words, right whales are big and fat!

Unlike many other large whales, right whales don't have a dorsal fin (the fin found on some whales' backs). They are baleen whales, which means that they don't have teeth. Instead, they filter tiny sea animals called copepods through fringed plates that hang from their upper jaw. Copepods are so tiny you could fit 500 of them in a single tablespoon.

Right whales eat as much as 750 kilograms (1,650 pounds) of this microscopic food in a single day. That adds up to over half a million calories daily! They need that much food to build up the blubber layer that keeps them warm in the frigid Atlantic waters, and helps them survive when food is scarce.

Identification

Researchers can tell one right whale from another by photographing the patterns of the callosities (wart-like bumps) on their heads. The heads of right whales are covered in these rough skin patches in many of the places that humans have hair. Callosities are found on top of the head, under the chin, and above the eyes. Each right whale has a unique pattern of callosities, making it easy for researchers to identify the whales. The  callosities are coloured by the many thousands of "whale lice" that live on them. These miniature creatures are more like tiny crabs than lice. They dig in the whale's skin and cling tightly so they don't fall off in the water. Whale lice can live only on the whale's body, and die if they fall off.

Migration

Many right whale mysteries remain unsolved. Scientists have discovered that right whales give birth to calves off the coasts of Florida and Georgia during the winter months. Most right whales disappear from human observation during this time. Then, during the late winter and early spring, they can be seen gathering in Cape Cod Bay and in other places off the coast of Massachusetts. By summer and into the fall months, a large number of right whales migrate to Canadian waters, where they are frequently observed in the Bay of Fundy and on the Scotian Shelf.

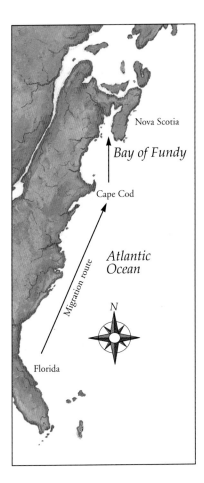

Whale Rescue Team

Because the right whale travels back and forth across the Canada/U.S. border, they must be monitored and protected from harm in both countries. In 1986, the North Atlantic Right Whale Consortium was formed to bring researchers together to collaborate on right whale science and conservation matters. In the face of increased threats to the right whale population, the Consortium has since strengthened its resolve to provide the North Atlantic right whale with the best possible chance for survival. Members of the Consortium include the New England Aquarium, the Center for Coastal Studies, the University of Rhode Island, Woods Hole Oceanographic Institution, East Coast Ecosystems, and other groups and individuals.

From the time the calves are born in U.S. waters in the winter, and during their travels up the eastern coast into Canadian waters, members of the Consortium are involved in various research and conservation projects in aid of this very rare whale. Among the projects underway are monitoring of the population in all habitat areas, and attempts to reduce human impact (from activities like fishing and shipping) on the whale.

East Coast Ecosystems

Founded in 1986 by Dr. Moira Brown, East Coast Ecosystems is a Canadian non-profit organization, whose primary concern is the fate of the North Atlantic right whale. Deborah Tobin is the Disentanglement Outreach Coordinator for

the organization, and is currently working to establish a whale emergency network in Maritime waters. In this photo, she is seen with pilot Jack Smith (far right) and aerial observer Darrin Sollows.

The Center for Coastal Studies

Since 1984, the Center for Coastal Studies in Provincetown, Massachusetts, has been freeing whales from life-threatening entanglements in fishing gear, using techniques developed by their staff. The Center maintains a research vessel, a patrol boat, a number of inflatable boats, and other specialized equipment for use in disentanglement.

Disentanglement experts like David and Stormy from the Center might be called upon to assist in a right whale entanglement in Canada, due to the rarity of the species.

Stormy & David

Dr. Charles "Stormy" Mayo is one of the founders of the Center for Coastal Studies, and has been a senior scientist there since 1976. Dr. Mayo is internationally known for his work with northern right whales and the habitat in which they live.

David K. Mattila has been a senior scientist with the Center since 1980. He is director of population studies, which maintains the largest database in the world on individually identified humpback whales. The photo below shows David (sitting) and Stormy during a rescue.